Temple Cat

by Andrew Clements ◆ *Illustrated by* Kate Kiesler

CLARION BOOKS/New York

Clarion Books
a Houghton Mifflin Company imprint
215 Park Avenue South, New York, NY 10003

The illustrations for this book were executed in oil paint.
The text is set in 18/24-point Phaistos.

For information about this and other Houghton Mifflin
trade and reference books and multimedia products,
visit The Bookstore at Houghton Mifflin on the World Wide Web
at (http://www.hmco.com/trade/).

Printed in Singapore

Library of Congress Cataloging-in-Publication Data

Clements, Andrew, 1949–
Temple cat / by Andrew Clements ; illustrated by Kate Kiesler.
p. cm.
Summary: A temple cat in ancient Egypt grows tired of being worshiped and cared for in a reverent fashion and travels to the seaside, where he finds genuine affection with a fisherman and his children.
ISBN 0-395-69842-1
[1. Cats—Fiction. 2. Egypt—Civilization—To 332 B.C.—Fiction.]
I. Kiesler, Kate A., ill. II. Title.
PZ7.C59118Te 1997
[E]—dc20
94-44082
CIP
AC

TWP 10 9 8 7 6 5 4 3 2 1

For my son, John
—*A. C.*

For Mom
—*K. K.*

In the ancient city of Neba there stood a temple,
and in the temple lived a cat.
But the cat did not just live there.
The cat was the lord of the temple.

Ever since he had been a tiny kitten
there had been servants
who did nothing else
but care for him and watch over him,
all day and all night.

They fed him.
They played music for him.
They danced for him.
They kept a sacred fire burning for him.

They worshiped him as a god.

No one could remember
when the people in this land
had started to worship cats,
and the cat certainly did not know or care.
All he knew
was that being the lord of the temple
was not much fun.

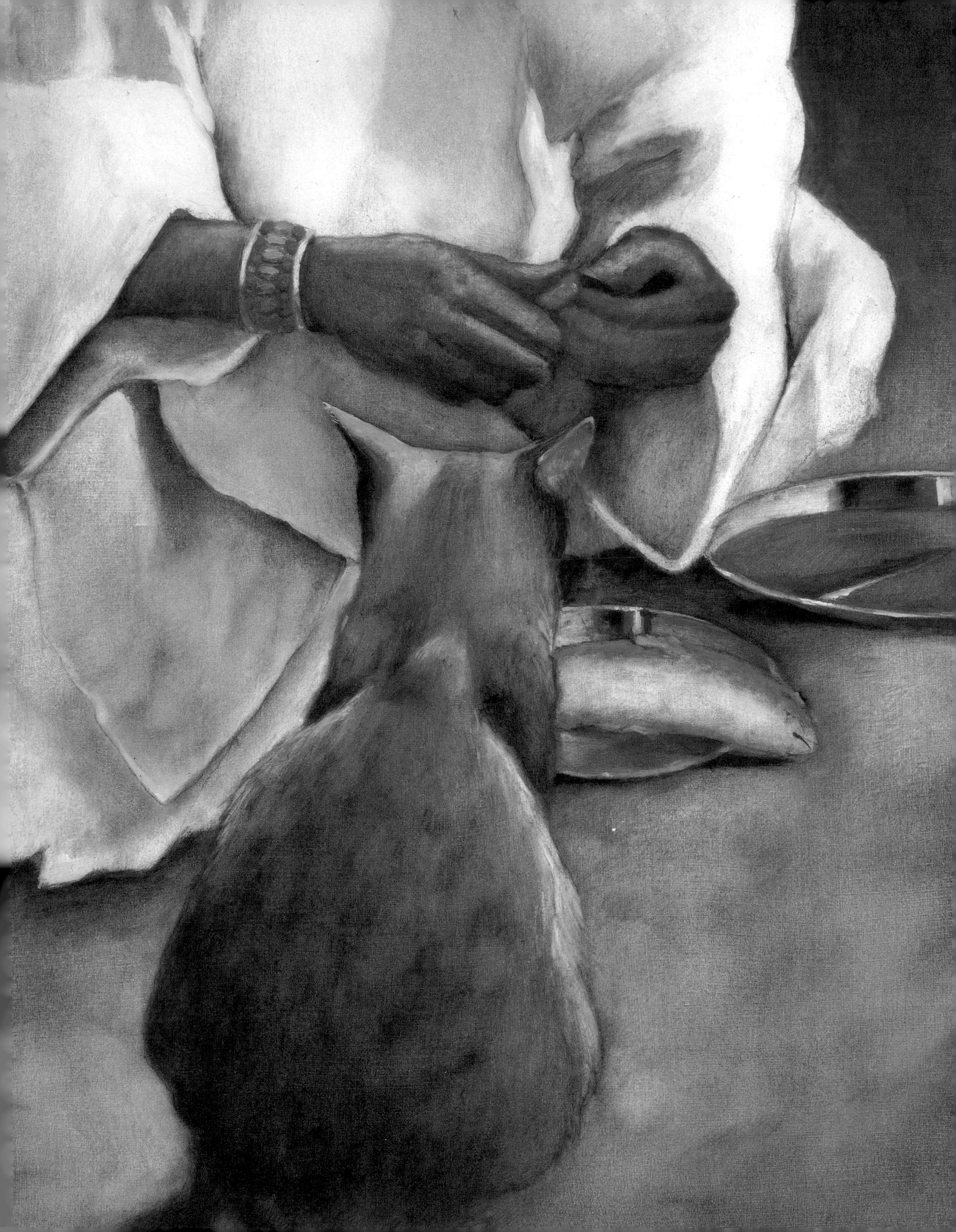

When he tried to catch a fish in the reflecting pool,
a servant would rush over and catch it for him,
and then cook it up with rich herbs and spices
and serve it to him in a little golden bowl.

If he stretched out to sleep in the sunshine
up on the cool stone of the windowsill,
a servant would gently lift him
and lay him back down
on the deep crimson pillows of his bed.

When he wanted to prowl around all alone at night
and catch the moths that flit in the moonlight
and scare himself silly with his own shadow,
a servant would follow him about with a fan and a torch
and spoil all the fun.

From his perch high above the courtyard,
past the reach of the tallest servant,
there in the highest branches of the almond tree,
he could see far beyond the temple walls.
There were children playing in the streets,
and all the other cats in the world roamed free.

So late one night,
he slipped out of the temple like a wisp of smoke.

First through the courtyard,
then down a lane, into an alley,
over a fence, across a field,
up a hill, through a pasture,
along a road, into a village—
and finally he came to rest
in a little barn as the sun was coming up.
And he slept as he had never slept before.

And he traveled this way for three more nights
until he came to the edge of a sea.

It was chilly,
and he went toward a little hut
where a smoky fire burned on the sand.

He moved cautiously into the ring of firelight and mewed.
The nights of traveling and not eating
had made him look scrawny and a little wild.
No one, not even his servants from the temple,
would have thought he was a god.

So the man who sat on the rough stool
tossed him a fish head.

For the first time in his life,
the little cat had a real cat supper.
And never had anything tasted so good.

And later when he purred
and rubbed against the fisherman's leg,
the man scratched behind his ears.
And never had anything felt so delicious.

Early the next morning the fisherman's children
came dancing out into the bright sunshine,
and then stopped in their tracks.

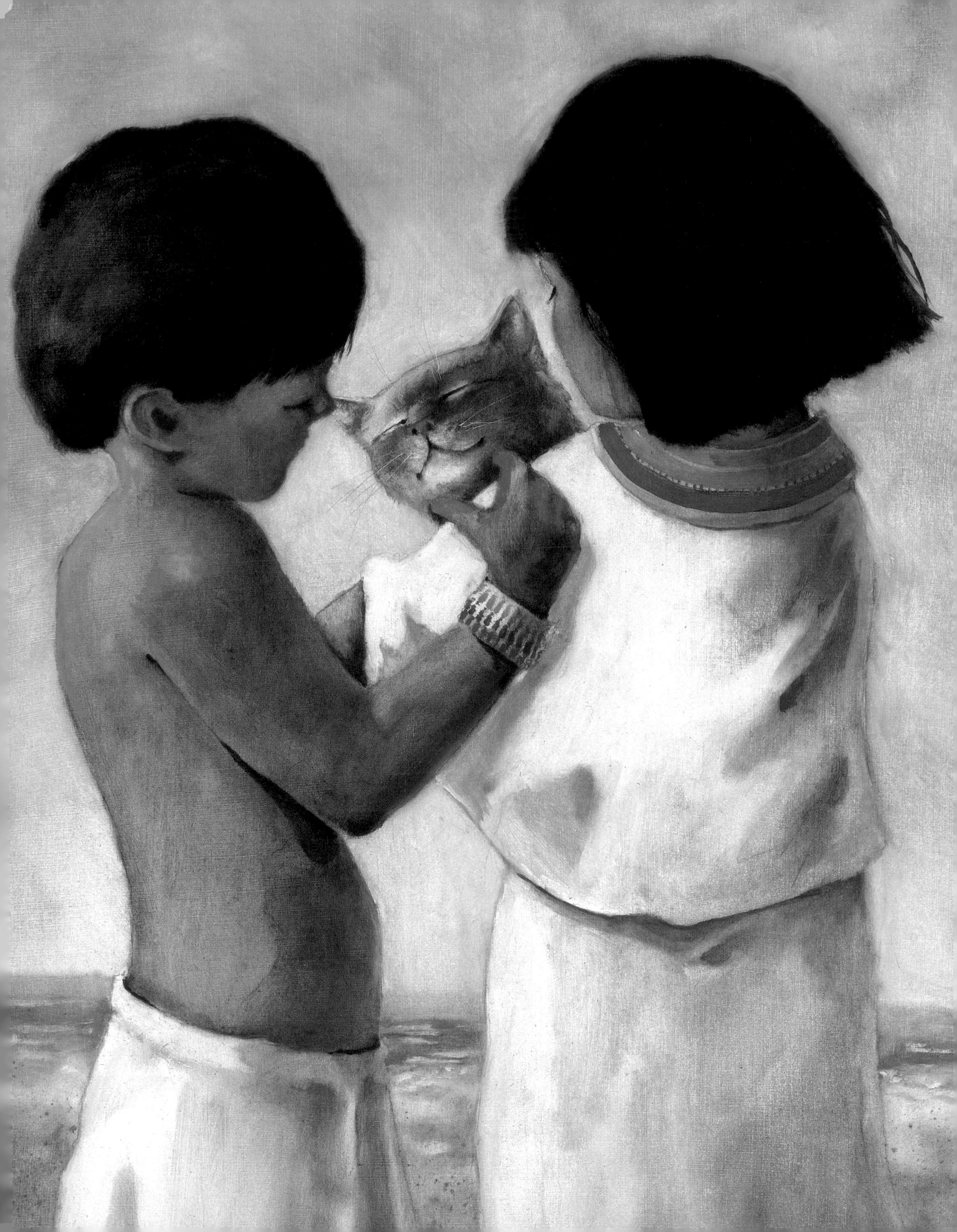

And then, before the cat even knew
what his dearest wish was,
it came true.
He played with the children,
and they loved him.